ALEX & ALEX

Written by Ziggy Hanaor   Illustrated by Ben Javens

This is Alex.

And this is Alex.

Sometimes Alex likes to dress up like a ballerina.

Sometimes Alex likes to dress up like a racing car driver.

Alex likes wearing wigs.

And Alex likes short hair.

Alex likes things to be in their place.

Alex likes making a mess in the kitchen.

Alex is good at building things.

Alex is also good at building things.

Sometimes they build things together.

Alex likes running and kicking a ball around.

Alex prefers reading and dreaming.

Alex and Alex go to the museum.

Alex loves looking at the pictures, but Alex is bored.
'Let's go,' says Alex, 'I'm hungry.'

Alex orders a burger.

Alex is vegetarian.

Alex is cross.

Alex and Alex have some alone time.

Alex likes to listen to music.

Alex likes to play computer games.

But Alex and Alex always make up.

Because Alex really, really, really, really, really, really, really, really, really...

...LIKES ALEX!

Alex & Alex

Text © Ziggy Hanaor
Illustration © Ben Javens

British Library Cataloguing-in-Publication Data.

A CIP record for this book is available from the British Library
ISBN: 978-1-80066-011-3

First published in the UK, 2021, in the USA, 2022

Cicada Books Ltd
48 Burghley Road
London, NW5 1UE
www.cicadabooks.co.uk

Printed in Poland